<u>Poems from the dead heart</u>

By Ved Prajapati

Indeed you may not like all the poems but you'll see the kind of growth a poet makes throughout a few years. For him the meaning, the matter of poetry often changes and that's what brought the changes in my poetry.

TABLE OF CONTENT:

<u>*Wishes*</u>

I need someone to listen to me, someone to talk to,
I'm not asking for more, just a cloudy night for us for a walk.

I see places filled with people though my heart shivers alone,
Second thoughts haunt me asking to kill me if I'm done.

Shh shut up what are you talking about, don't ;
Yeah, they talk like they will take care next time yet I know they won't

Down to my last breath, it's all me alone inside;
Seeing the crowd getting upset finding new places just to hide

<u>*The Night fell*</u>

The night came, my smile dropped, and I was in bed.
Thinking about someone, about tomorrow, while fighting demons in my head

The night fell, I remembered things, and the guilt took over.
Thinking about where it went wrong, was it in October?

The night fell, and I got lost in my thoughts—scenes I wish were true.
People left. Yeah, they left, but to be honest, it's what I already knew.

The night fell, and the demons came to play their games.
My mind is dying, my soul is crying, and my heart is burning to the flames

The night fell, and I was awake, having no one or nowhere to go.
The morning came early. I'm sad, but I'll just smile, just for show.

Sensitive?

The words that pleased me someday today pierce through my heart.

The acts of kindness I felt were done because they were just pity.

The people who once made me smile are the ones making me overwhelmed.

The mistakes I thought were there were just my fault.

I'm afraid to go out; the anxiety now loves me, I guess.

I'm afraid to speak my mind because they would judge me, I guess.

I'm afraid to relive moments again. I'll just cry now, I guess.

I'm afraid to trust someone new. I just have issues with everything, I guess.

Just thinking

Just thinking if the stars gaze at us the way we do,

Or if the moon too smiles, thinking about us?

Just thinking if the rose ever wonders how beautiful and sweet it is,

Or if the oceans too feel relief hearing the water that flows.

Just thinking if the broken glass hurts itself too,

Or if the stabbing knife ever wonders whose blood it is.

Just thinking if time feels it's too fast or too slow sometimes,

Or if the night too feels peaceful alone, all by itself.

Just thinking if anything ever makes any sense,

Or we just accept things, believing them as an incomplete poem.

<u>*What are empty feelings?*</u>

It's like you're so sad that you are forced to smile.

 Always so charming that no one knows you could even cry

It's like being the leaf that's left alone on rainy days.

All by itself, so isolated, so lonely, left alone there; dry

It's like being lively enough to laugh with others.

Yet dead enough to not even be able to shed a tear.

It's being courageous enough to fight something like "anxiety."

Yet I'm scared enough to even open up and talk when someone's near.

Indeed, it's like dancing in the rain in sunny weather.

Feeling everything yet nothing so much yet so little altogether

Is it bad?

Is it bad to stay up late every night

Or is it good because you find peace late then

Is it bad not to speak of your mind

Or is it food because everyone's doing the same thing

Is it bad always faking a smile

Or is it good because no one ever notices

Is it bad always thinking too much

Or is it good because you know what can ruin you

Is it good, anything I ever do

or is it just something no one does or ever will care about.

<u>**_Path Of life_**</u>

The path of life I'm walking on, I find it difficult to follow.

Where does it lead me? I'm not sure. Where would I end up? I don't know.

The path of life I see has no unerring turns; indeed, I see

Every turn has a story, and every story looks unfinished to me.

The path of life I've chosen feels too overwhelming, I guess.

Everything I get on the journey isn't perfect, neither more nor less.

The path of life I follow shows me not much but little things.

I walk on the trails I see and step on every thorn that stings.

On the path of life, I wish I could find the stars I'm looking for.

I wish I could see every subtle sign that shows me my flaws.

<u>*Me*</u>

I am the scariest dream, of which I'm too afraid.

I am haunted by the past, which I chose to forget.

I am an unspoken thought, which I often drown in too.

I am scared of thinking too much, thinking about what can't be said.

I am an unreal moment, which neither I want to feel.

I am frightened of the feelings, which were supposed to make me happy.

I am the words not chosen, which I too feel are hurtful sometimes.

I am against these non violence, which used to make ne feel safe.

I am indeed an unfinished poetry, which I too want to leave.

I am indeed that incomplete story, the story I chose to keep.

<u>*Needs*</u>

I too need to get these voices of my head speak to let them shout;

I too need someone's, shoulder someone's shoulder to cry out;

I too need someone to hear my nonsense and the things I talk about;

I too need some time from Overthinking some time from self doubt;

I also want to live happily;

To smile , to talk merrily;

But I just think too much unnecessarily;

I just think this is the reality sadly.....

It'll be okay

It'll be okay, but the memories won't go
It'll be okay, but you'll have a bad side to show.

It'll be okay, but the scars won't go; they'll be there.
It'll be okay, but people won't always be there for you to care.

It'll be okay, but it'll hurt you, I know.
It'll be okay, but it will haunt you, though.

It'll be okay, but I'm sure you'll have to wait a bit.
It'll be okay. I hope it'll be better than just quitting.

It'll be okay, but you'll have to bear the pain somehow.
It'll be okay. I promise it's just here for now.

<u>*How Do You?*</u>

How do you run away from things in your head?

Run away from something so sad that it doesn't let you think.

Run away, but when because it's my shadow following me?

How do you stop thinking about sadness?

Stop thinking that you're someone who just deserves these things.

Stop thinking everyone will leave doubt or forget you.

How do you become happy?

Become happy when you're lonely, thinking about everything that is wrong.

Be happy when a single thought can change your whole day.

How can you be someone you thought you'd never be?

Someone who smiles when it hurts and laughs when he wants to cry out loud,

someone who is so sad that it depresses everyone else around him?

THE ANSWERS

"Let me tell you the answers you've been begging for from everyone

You're not desperate maybe you're just questioning why things ever began"

The joy? "Yes you do deserve better but you found comfort in the sadness you live in

The fake smiles and the lying you're fine have made you believe it in

The heart? "It's one of the purest things it feels for everyone except you I guess

You spend more time crying with the moon instead of focusing on progress

The cries and the sleep? "You love to sleep you say it what something loved by your heart

No, You love to fall asleep because of the fear of falling apart

It's never been as difficult as you make it's just the fear of sadness my friends

Now you have the answers it's on you what you do You're the one on whom it depends

Overthinking

My mind isn't a friend of mine these days. He's keeping me busy.

I guess the kid He's dying inside, but he isn't crying, is he?

I keep thinking of things over and over again. Can I see the future?

Well, I guess I can, because everything I think happens later or sooner.

I thought of my friends not being friends with me. I guess they found someone better.

I guess I was the 'BORING' one. Yes, that's why I didn't matter.

Am I annoying them? Are they mad at me? Why aren't they talking like they used to?

'FOREVER' would just be a word for me; well, who knew?

Are they my friends, or am I forcing them to talk? I don't think they hear

Well, that's my trauma right there, folks—the anxieties and the fear.

<u>*SO CLOSE, YET SO FAR*</u>

I was so close to sleeping, yet so far from my dreams.

My heart was too close to crying, yet too far for the screams.

The moon was so close to hug me, yet so far away to see.

My mind was too close to dying, yet too far from me.

The rain was so close to hit me, yet so far to fall.

My soul was too close to leave yet too desperate to call.

The stars were so close to touch yet so far away to die.

My eyes were too close to rain yet too far away to cry.

The sky was so close to love me yet so far to explain.

I was too close to breaking down, yet too far from the pain.

<u>*Two Souls*</u>

It is sad to tell you about the bad weather.

A story of two lovers who can't be together

The distance between them kept them separated.

What they once loved about themselves is now something they hate.

them seeing each other cry, hoping it could get better,

forgetting about what they got—the love and the letters.

One day, one of them decided to never see the other.

breaking the promises they made about staying with one another.

The moon saw the two souls leaving, but the two hearts still bonded too tight.

None of them showed up that day. The only one crying was Night.

Thinking out tiredly

I'm tired, to be honest. It's just making me sad every day.
If I were to have the choice to be okay with a condition
I would make the choice regardless of the condition.
It was always my fault, I know.
But aren't humans made to learn from mistakes?
Maybe these things got me overthinking.
but I truly know it's just because I know I'm replaceable.
Things were good, I think, until I learned people leave.
Things were good until crying was only for toys.
Things were supposed to be good; maybe I grew mature from pain.

<u>*With her*</u>

The stars shining above us are sleeping peacefully.
No need for meditation, just her, and no therapy.

Wanna play just music? Yeah, all night long.
No need for the world, just me and her all along.

Just looking into her eyes, I watched her smile all night.
Yeah, I'm not okay now, but I swear I'll be alright.

I'll listen to her stories about how her day was.
I would have problems, but I'll put them away.

I know it's not true. I know I'm just overthinking.
But if it can come true, I'll be there without even thinking.

Losing Himself

After losing himself, he found peace of mind.
Finding the solutions, with the worries left behind

Losing his smile, he found the tears.
In finding the right path, he forgot his fears.

Losing the charm in his eyes, he found the good
Finding the reality of the world, he did what he should.

No doubt he fell; his own people were with him every single time.
Telling people it's okay to be sad sometimes

He is thankful to everyone who mattered.
Thankful because they were there when his life shattered.

Growing Night

The nights I saw grew older, and the angel was crying for happiness; no one told her ever.
The stars I saw were breaking, and the moments were breathtaking.

It was never easy for me; I thought I'd get over it. The pain grew, yeah, just a little bit.
It'll get better. It's what they say; I'll just need a little motivation, and I'll find a way.

It's not easy. I should accept that for sure, but I'll somehow get out, I assure you.

I'm sure I'll be better. not today, maybe tomorrow, I'll be better of my pains at last, Im sure I know

Let's talk with the Moon

Let's talk with the moon once again, shall we?
Let's normalize the fears and tears they can be.

Let's talk with the moon, discussing those scary nights.
Maybe he will listen to us and our untold fears.

Let's talk with the moon and say we're really sorry.
Promising we'll get better and we won't worry

Let's talk with the moon. We can show him the side that can't be shown.
He won't judge us; instead, he'll be there when we're crying alone.

Let's talk with the moon one last Time before he leaves.
Let's try one more time what we left or failed now that he too believes

Broken Dream

I woke up panting past my bed and didn't know the watery eyes
I heard someone sobbing beside the bench. I heard those pretty cries.

It was a dream. I somewhat knew that in my mind.
I saw myself crying when I saw the person beside me.

The dream, I guess, got me scared and maybe sad too.
I wanted to wipe those tears away, but it was a dream only I knew.

I turned myself around. I saw the trauma memories hitting
I was still crying in the dream, but I felt like I was sinking.

I woke up panting from that dream and didn't know the tears
I saw it was me crying beside her, crying because of my fears.

<u>*With the rain*</u>

With the rain, the clouds are crying for the touch they never got.
The moon is hiding herself, trying not to get caught.

With the rain, I saw the trees; they looked sad.
The birds were trying to find someone—someone they never had.

With the rain, I heard my heart cracking, breaking, and falling.
The heart was screaming and begging for help; it was crawling.

With the rain, I saw the past, but I wasn't counting the stars.
Searching for the smiles—the smiles I left too far

With the rain, I wiped away the tears. I guess nothing can be done.
The clouds tried to hide the so-called brightening sun.

Addiction

**Is it like your favorite song, heard not for minutes but hours long,

Something right, yet something wrong, or do my memories prolong?**

**Is it watching your favorite show, waiting outside for it to snow,

Us getting eager to know, or me being your friend or a foe?**

**Is it reading your favorite book, moments when the butterflies in the stomach shook,

Or the places where the characters took, or imagining how pretty you look?**

**Is it playing with your best friend, crying when the movies end,

Or being where nostalgia sends, or looking away to just pretend?**

Whispering in the ears

Whispering in the ear, what did the earth tell?
My dear, you're living the life of a lost soul, feeling like hell.

Whispering in the ears, what did the waterfall show?
My dear, you're planting a tree whose seed you should never sow.

Whispering in the ear, what did the leaves bleed?
My dear, asking for poison in the garden of medicine you need.

Whispering in the ear, what did the trees in spring shed?
My dear, searching for tears and smiles on the faces of the dead.

Whispering in the ear, what did the mother say in the end?
My dear, always live to love, even with only seconds to spend.

<u>*Want to go*</u>

I just want to go and get lost somewhere in the mountains.
Somewhere, where the moon never dawns and loneliness never reigns

I just want to go and fly somewhere high in the sky, among the clouds.
Somewhere, where the hatred doesn't follow, the heart can shout.

I just want to go and hide in the forest, in between the trees.
Somewhere, where the music is the waterfall and the buzzing bees

I just want to go and get forgotten by everyone forever.
Somewhere, where only the rain speaks, the mind can surrender.

I just want to go and take my life for granted for a while.
Somewhere, no one remembers where I can really smile.

<u>*They said*</u>

You don't talk much, they said. Tell this to the flowers. I always cry with

You must be everyone's favorite. They said, Ask this to the bed I lie with.

You smiled too much, they said, Tell this to the moon. I complain to.

You never tell anyone anything;they said, Tell this to the clouds, which I explain to

You are so strong, they said. Tell this to the trees who saw my mourning heart.

You never said no; they said tell this to the tears, wanting me to fall apart.

You always look confident. They said, Tell this to the pillow who saw me break.

You always make us laugh. They said, Tell this to my blanket, who saw the other half.

You write sad poems about suffering. They asked why; ask this to... Let it be.

There's no one to ask. I'm fine; it's the way I want to be.

<u>*Pick Your Poison*</u>

Pick your poison. Will it be the crying heart or the negative mind?
Or you prefer being sad when there's happiness to find.

Pick your poison. Will it be doubting questions or underconfident screams?
Or you prefer sleeping when there are people chasing your dreams.

Pick your poison. Will it be the darkness you cause or the light you ignore?
Or you prefer asking for water when it's raining near the shore.

Pick your poison. My friend, will it be a ticking clock or a cup of caffcinc?
Or you prefer being silent whcn it's your turn to charm in the scene.

Pick your poison, my mate. You have no more left in the pocket, I see.
It's up to you to decide what you do and what you'll even be.

<u>*Anxiety is a book*</u>

Anxiety is my book, the way I pen down my sorrow.
To write is a disease, though so is hoping for tomorrow.

Anxiety is my book, the way I tear the pages I don't like,
Though I end up in the dark where everything looks alike.

Anxiety is my book, the way I scribble away my smiles,
Yet I know I'll be sad even after my best times.

Anxiety is my book, the way I crave it to be a little nice,
Though I want to get rid of it thinking about my vices.

Anxiety is my book, my foe, my friend at last indeed,
I know every time I'll break down crying for what I need.

What is poetry?

Is it just words bleeding on paper?
Or a broken heart crying in a stanza?
Is it to pen down what you can't say?
Or is it just writing with tears?

Is it a cheerful smile gathered on a page?
Or beautiful memories written by love?
Is it scribbling nostalgia with a pen?
Or is it just smiling and looking at a line?

Is it that overwhelming pain of leaving written
Or is it that underwhelming thought that can't be spoken?
Is it overthinking lines written by a person?
Or is it just depressing words by someone we call a poet?

Is the feeling of falling in love simplified?
Or are the butterflies in love written down?
Is it the delusion we wish were true on a page?
Or just a few lines that explain us better than ourselves?

Is it each and every emotion not thought of on paper?
Or is it the smiling and crying of a person in words?
Everything indeed is poetry.
Be it first love or last breath.

<u>*Truth or lies?*</u>

I don't need the truth anymore.
For me, the lies would suffice now.
I don't need those harsh truths to live. As of now, I ask you to bury me in the lies.

Heal me with the lies that feel good. Even if the truth seems to be more believable.
I would love to smile at the lies.
Rather than crying over the truth, I can't change

Give me the sunset of lies that dawn passes me.
I won't care if the sunrise of truth has more light.
I'm tired of the truth that stings me.
As of now, I'll happily drink the poison of lies. That kills me slowly.

I won't ask you to stay with me anymore.
I would believe anything you say to leave.
 Just for one last time, I'll ask youWhat hurts more, the truth or the lies?

Birds of the Tree

The raven is making noises in the pond near the tree.
The bluebird left there waiting to be found and set free.

The Raven took a bath in the water, coming out when I felt it was gone.
The bluebird hid in its nest as I saw it set to dawn.

The raven kept on circling the tree, going around the domes.
The bluebird stayed down the tree, and with broken wings, it roamed.

The Raven one day fell, and the pebble of happiness hurt its wings.
The bluebird seemed to rise and fly, forgetting the sadness the past brings.

The Raven didn't die but lay peacefully, seeing the flowers on the tree bloom.
The Bluebird saw it fainting, surviving with the broken wings and making its
tomb.

Love Indeed

Love is the happiness I found in you and the smiles I got from you.
It is the sadness you left me and things that weren't true.

Love is poetry. I wrote to you about the dreams I wish would come true.
It is the thing I want, wanting you to stay too.

Love is the song you like. The song I sing for you
It was the melodies we made that we decided to dance to.

Love is the time we spend and the small efforts we put in to
It is the promise we made and planned to keep too.

Love is nothing; it is not even that good. This says who?
Indeed, love is the most beautiful feeling I felt and I wish you felt too.

<u>Metaphorical Irony</u>

You say the eyes don't lie,
Then why didn't you understand mine when they were blood red?

You say time heals everything,
Then why do the scars seem more hurtful?

You say life's a song, and I get to write the lyrics.
Then why does every melody I live feel like a noise?

You say the weight of yesterday is lighter than the joy of today.
Then why do people kill the present with the fear of tomorrow?

Indeed, life isn't always a metaphor we listen to.
Indeed, it is the irony we have to dance through.

<u>*Cosmos and Me*</u>

How can you not tell that my mind is an entire cosmos within?
When everything inside is a shattering star.

The eyes resemble the moon, so cold and dry, waiting for water.
And the heart is burning like the sun in space.

The memories in which I remember every Constellation
And the shaking hands seem like trembling cosmic strings.

The blood on my hand looks like a meteor that could hurt.
And the anger I hide is like the planets on the other side.

How do you not see my mind as an entire universe?
When every star connects to one place, that's the home it's searching for.

Dying Rose

A dying rose, I found in my book,
The book that hasn't been touched since an era.

The dying rose I saw, withered with dryness, begging for water—
For the water that once flourished it wholeheartedly.

The dying rose, with some petals that lost their fragrance a while ago,
The fragrance that once called every bee in the house.

The dying rose seems like it's still breathing,
Breathing as if it wants to live, even after the tragedy.

The dying rose I took in my hands, the thorns were too brittle to hurt.
It still gave me a scar big enough to regret the dying rose.

Do I ruin everything I touch?

Be it the rose that withered in the palm of your hand that just wanted to feel
itBe it the trust I've broken with my words that meant no harm

Be it the glass I broke in my hands by holding it tight Enough
Be it the help that someone asked, which turned into a disaster.

Be it the time of the people who wished for Nothing
Be it the lies I told that turned into hurtful truths

Be it anything I do with the intention of good
Be it my smiles I turned into cries by thinking too much.

Be it my mind I ruined myself by thinking I never deserved happiness.
Be it myself, I destroyed it just to live peacefully.

<u>*Poetry of Nature*</u>

The poetry of nature is the birds singing about the lines.
The melodies we hear, rather than feeling the soothing gestures and signs.

The poetry of nature is the moon that dances along the stars all night.
The steps we see, rather than thinking about what they convey or what they might be,.

The poetry of nature is the mesmerizing sunset that writes of its charm.
The shining we often look at, rather than looking at what is good and what does harm,

The poetry of nature is all along the path, whistling through your ears.
The beauty we often listen to, rather than thinking and pondering what we hear.

The poetry of nature is indeed what has been with you all along.
It is indeed the poetry nature sings, and the words dance along.

<u>*Unfinished Poetry*</u>

The unfinished poem rested there on the desk all alone.
 The broken quill there was having a complete poetry to mourn.

With a few things written, it seems like a few lines on a page.
The spilled ink there told me about the poem and its age.

A few torn pages lie on the ground, all sad and ripped apart.
 The resting sun there told me about the poet who went long afar.

 A dying rose lay beneath, hidden well, just out of sight.
The coffee cup, half empty, told me everything about that night.

I saw a diary on the side, with nothing but scribbles all over.
It was nothing less than a love story with yet another broken lover.

<u>*Nowhere*</u>

In the middle of nowhere, I stare at the stars just for a while.
 Waiting for myself to get better and walk on the empty road with a smile.

In the middle of nowhere, I'm stuck gazing at the night forever.
Waiting for my old self to come back and see him give up and surrender.

In the middle of nowhere, where there's nothing to look for,
Waiting for myself to move on, just to come back to where I was before.

In the middle of nowhere, I know I can't move any further ahead.
Waiting for the stars to come back and talk to me and ask why I am sad.

In the middle of nowhere, will I ever run anywhere now?
I guess I'm just waiting for myself to somehow make me move.

<u>*At that moment*</u>

At that moment, I fell for the eyes looking at me.
Those eyes felt like the world I wanted to see.

At that moment, that one smile felt like an eternity.
That one smile seemed like a shooting star in a broken city.

At that moment, I felt the stars that plucked my heart.
The stars seemed to wipe away my tears, which were falling apart.

At that moment, I saw the sun collide in the back of my mind.
At that moment, though, I wished for time to slow down and fall a little behind.

Poetry and Realism

Poetic is the night where the moon chose not to smile.
Realistic, though, are the stars that went missing for a while.

Poetic are the smiles that we left when we grew up and apart.
Realistic though is the sadness that chose to follow us so long and so far.

Poetic are the birds that went away, missing forever someday.
Realistic, though, are the chirping memories we still hear the same way.

Poetic is the poison that we drink every day with the hope of healing.
Realistic, though, is the medicine resting right there, with an unsaid feeling.

Poetic is the pen with which I wrote the lines that turned into poetry.
Realistic, though, are the emotions all inside waiting to be set free.

<u>*Still there*</u>

I'll still be there watching you leave, just in case you need me.
I'll be standing on the path where we left each other.

I'll be the moon who looks at you all the time without you knowing.
I'll still be there, with the stars waiting for you.

I'll be crying right there on the road. We said goodbye for the last time.
I'll still forgive you if you tell me you want to come back.

I'll still be there, watering the flowers we kept there, someday.
I'll still give you those flowers if we ever meet again.

I'll still be waiting for you, for us, for everything we ever had.
I'll still be waiting just to make sure you're okay and smiling.

<u>*I thought*</u>

I thought I loved the bird I had in the cage until I set him free from the cage and watched it fly happily.

I thought I was okay holding the shattered glasses in my hand, but when I let the glass go from my hand, I felt a little less pain.

I thought it was okay that people were hurting my heart, but then I let them go from my life and found it a little bit more peaceful.

I thought it'd be good to have as many friends as possible, yet when I let a few go who never came back, I found the true ones.

I thought holding on to everything was life, but now I get it; it's the art of letting go of what's called life.

Staring out the window

See the birds over there. In 1, 2, and 3, there are
I see 2 of them happy on the 3rd alone so far.

See the stars in the sky, counting till the numbers end.
I see the raven coming out of the pond. It was someone to befriend.

See the moon in between the clouds, only one, alone like us.
I hear the sweet promises everyone kept; they don't remember, and no one does.

See the trees over there. There are only a few to count and a few to see.
I hear children playing there and the soul wanting to be free.

See the man over there, standing alone in the crowd?
I guess it's me, with the thoughts in my mind, never so loud.

<u>*Emotions*</u>

What is anger?
Is it punching the wall until the wrists hurt?
Or is it the heart hurting when things don't go as planned?

What is happiness?
Is it smiling, laughing, and getting joyful once in a while?
Or is it when the heart knows everything is alright?

What is anxiety?
Is it trembling when the earthquake arrives?
Or is it being scared when there's nothing to worry about?

What is nostalgia?
Is it remembering the good things about the past?
Or is it feeling sentimental when you see everything happy around you?

What is sadness?
Is it crying when there's nothing okay?
Or is it the heart trying to lighten itself with the tears?

A GOODBYE FROM A GHOST

"I died a while ago, and I was not sad. Just careless," he said.
"I should've been more careful. I could've been with them instead."

"One goodbye to those who kept me nearer to their hearts.
One goodbye to those who'd never let me fall apart."

"One goodbye to my mom. I wish I slept on her lap.
One goodbye to my dad, who made me strong; I would never snap."

"One goodbye to the love I wish I found sooner.
One goodbye to the friends who made my life semilunar."

"I wish I still lived for a few moments before I would go.
I wish I loved them more, more than I would show."

<u>*Thoughts*</u>

It feels like I'm drowning in my own thoughts.
If I go too deep, everything goes black.
But there's no hope of swimming back up either.

It feels like I'm being choked by myself.
If I let myself go, I'll probably kill myself.
But if I don't, I will be here forever.

It feels like I'm falling into my own dreams.
If I reach the end, I will be heartless.
But having a heart is hurting too.

It feels like I'm getting numb in my sleep.
If I let it, I won't be able to get up.
But if I don't, I have to wake up again.

It feels like I'm running from myself lately.
If I went far away, I would be lost.
But if I don't, there's nothing left for me.

I GAVE MYSELF

I saw a boy sitting sad on the road, sitting with the future alone.
I gave him my childhood, and as of now, there's a heart burdened with stone.

I saw an old lady walking by the path, walking with fear along
I gave her my optimism, but as of now, it all seems to be going just wrong.

I saw a young man upset about life, crying, all tired.
I gave him my laughs, and as of now, the tears stay by my side.

I saw a baby born and crying, having a full life left unattended.
I gave it my happy moments; as of now, it's just guilt I befriended.

I saw the world, all different now, and it all seemed strange.
I gave myself to it just to know some things never change.

<u>**When You're not enough.**</u>

I acknowledge I'm not the best; I'm sorry,
My friends around me always make me worry.

Not a perfect nose, nor the eye you seek,
Every single day, each taunt feels bleak.

"Shh, your voice is so bad; don't talk with us,"
You too have imperfections; why should I adjust?

"You need to change," laughing at me, no one stopped,
The little bit of confidence I had, from my head, was chopped.

What did you give me? Some shivers and some pain,
I apologize for talking; I won't be here again.

ALL IN MY HEAD

Is it all just in my head, or is the moon a charm?
Is it all a delusion because the traumas harm?

Is it all in my head, or are the thoughts really this scary?
Is it my imagination because the heart feels too heavy?

Is it all in my head, or are the screams getting loud?
Is it myself because I seem to be lost in this broken crowd?

Is it all in my head, or are the trees withering this fast?
Is it a dream because the mind seems to rewind the past?

Is it all in my head because I wish nothing were true?
Is it my reality or something I'm going through?

<u>*SMILING*</u>

Smiling because the tears won't come rumbling down the eyes,
Laughing because the sadness numbs and the thought dies.

Smiling because it's easier than speaking your mind,
The thoughts that run inside left me forever.

Smiling because I'm not perfect; I am bad, I know,
Laughing with them because there's nothing else to show.

Smiling because they hate me, I too, I guess,
Laughing at myself because I never express.

Smiling because... eh, nothing matters to me anymore,
Laughing because, because it remains as it was before.

Echoes in an Abandoned House

What do I find in a house so abandoned, so old?
where the words too fail to explain the antiquity
The dust on the desk often echoes a story untold.
The paintings that were always heard lost their dignity.

The windows are so cracked that the doves refuse to visit.
I hear the door scream and cry in echoes of isolation.
How is it too perfect for you? I see it as so explicit.
No one belongs to the house nor is ever damned on this creation.

I hear what they say. Echoes of the old soul, remembering times
How do the quill and paper get up by themselves to hear them?
What they did together was called poetry with pretty lines.
The ghost too shed tears on the house so old; they condemn

Indeed, What Echoes is the poet who never got anything he wished for.
He, the poet, often echoes his past, which he sometimes mourns over.
Indeed, he left only the echoes there—nothing less nor something more.
Now the house has been abandoned, waiting and hoping for closure.

A broken car on an unsung road

With a loss of hope and rust on the car, I stay stranded on the unsung road.
With a few leaves to drop and a few drops to fall, I stay lonely all alone.

With no song to play or melody to sing, I remain silent on the unsung road.
With a few droplets of poison and a sense of love, I start walking home.

With the colors so dim and clouds around, I hide the tears behind my eyes.
With the stars yet to shine and no idea of myself, I hope the eyes will lie.

With no rain above and no roof to trust, I blame the unsung road somehow.
With no idea of going home or where to run, I won't get peace anyhow.

With the no pole that says home around, I torture myself afar.
With days to pass and yet a lifetime to live, I wander the unsung road for
now.

<u>*Half drunk Wine*</u>

The half drunk Wine that rests there on the table beside her man
He,who takes yet another sip, lights his cigarette in his old dark den

With his hand on paper with poetry to his love,he decides to drown in curse
The half drunk Wine mourns for her man,who's waiting for the worse.

With Glass half empty though eyes half full, He waits for thee, who won't come
He yet prays in the smoke he breathes, drinks though more hoping to get numb

One life in hand and one withered in his heart, He sees the Glass to be her
She too was a poison, slow yet stronger one, He thinks as he starts to stir

The glass indeed emptied, the tears yet to come wipe the sadness he sleeps there and then
Hoping for her to be in his dreams to give her the poem, and promise to never drink again.

Whispers of the wine

The girl sat there, shadows of tears whispering beneath her lips.
The way she dawns her eye close, an indeed peaceful eclipse

She then lifted her quill, half broken, half unready to write again.
Indeed, she lifted the glass of wine, swallowing the sorrows of her man.

The tear that falls goes with the ink there to write heartbreak.
She pours the wine on the floor, sweeping and spilling her mistakes.

The cigarette she picks has a scent she feels as she sparks.
Thinking about what has and could go wrong, she breaks as she marks

With the wine falling and rain in her eyes, she lies in her world.
She sees her tears that fell on the paper. Watch getting impearled.

<u>*Moonlit tears*</u>

I saw the way you kept your head down, waiting for the tears nevertheless.
Only I know how I begged them, God, to bring your heart back to esse.

Your eyes are edged by the pearls of your tears and the innocence of your charm.
Only I know what they said, how they never lied, and whether they meant any harm.

The way you spoke, how I listened to it, and how I felt everything you said
Only I know what your heart has to say. They said it was nothing but dead.

The way you laid on my shoulders, I felt the world to be with me, and even more.
Only I know how you made me feel being here, like the moonlight on a sad seashore.

Indeed, you left the porch. We once used to sit and talk about what and what not.
Only I was once scared of the moon being too good and indeed getting caught.

<u>*Haunted by your smile*</u>

What became of the home that once had us talking all day long?
Listening to the tune of us, fighting yet loving over right and wrong

Indeed, I'm being haunted by your smile, the smile I used and still adore.
The way you smiled, Thee's eyes said everything you couldn't say sitting
ashore.

I still hear your voice. Oh, how that voice made me love you all again.
The way you made the promises, only I believed they were true, and then

How I'm still haunted by your presence with thee's empty arms for me
I still have the memories, I think of them often, I pray would die before me.

Still haunted by your eyes that once searched for me in the house left alone.
Still haunted by the future we thought of—indeed, the dreams you used to
show

<u>*The Melancholy of You*</u>

The Melancholy of Us is indeed that I'm still waiting here for you.
With rain, yet I see my eyes dry and longing, waiting to adore you.

The Melancholy of Rain is indeed the time I spend thinking of you.
Oh to be cursed by the clouds though, called down just to love you

The melancholy of the moon is not seeing us together anymore in no time.
How indeed it can't just be me this way, forgetting our poetry and rhyme.

The melancholy of sunset, not wanting to see us the way we are, indeed
It sees our porch as empty, where only happiness used to bleed.

The melancholy of you is indeed not wanting us, or just me, I guess.
Oh, what have I become of myself? I am indeed just "a poet in distress."

<u>*The Letter Never Sent*</u>

What all I have left is this letter never sent, the words it held were words never spent
With a past that haunts and a future that tortures, I'm sitting here with a broken present.

The ink has started to fade, with the love it conveyed, and the fears it portrayed
The rose I kept to tell the stories has mourned, now withered and decayed.

The quill now often cries over this calamity, seeing me in my weakening sanity
The world within the letter I failed to send often witnesses my quiet inanity.

The paper too begins to intensify, the memories I struggle to identify
Whether this was indeed heartbreak or just a broken poet, I cannot specify.

Indeed I wish I never wrote the letter now, or that she might receive it somehow
With this heart still hoping for some things, but some things never reach thou.

<u>The Letter Never Received</u>

The letter, so it never came indeed,
The words kept hidden I never got to read.
Was it silence that broke us apart,
Or the things we had but freed from the heart?

I often open the windows for you,
To get the letter from thee, but to who?
Indeed, was the love ever for me, I wonder,
Or were the promises ever true, I ponder?

At the porch, I sit waiting once in a while,
It's been so long without you and your smile.
I wish you could just come back,
For once, maybe, and sit beside me for a while.

I won't and can't cry to the moon now too,
It says it can't see me like this, without you.
Not seen you in this while, I often wonder,
Were you ever real, or was the sky never blue?

Indeed, you're my life in my hands I've lost,
You were the happiness that I never accost.
Why then, indeed, am I forgetting myself?
Was it ever worth it? Ever worth this cost?

<u>**Thank you**</u>

Thank you so much for everything you did,
For being, on my side every time I fell;
My lips were too tired to even tell;
Every sad day you made my day so well;
Every time you changed my life back from hell;
Thank you, maybe it's less to convey in words.....
But thank you for helping me out
Letting my heart shout
Every time I had doubt
Every time my life became a drought...
Thank you for everything...